I0723793

The Bachelors and Widows Christmas Party

Audrey J. Whitson

The Bachelors and Widows Christmas Party

Radical Bookshop and Press
4838 Richard Road SW, Suite 300
Calgary, AB T3E 6L1

© 2023 Audrey J. Whitson

FIC029000 - Fiction, Short Stories

Editors: Lexie Angelo
Cover Design: Lexie Angelo

ISBN-13: 978-1-990201-15-8

Printed in the United States

*For Busby, Alberta, my hometown,
which has never had a B&W Xmas party,
but has all the characters for one.*

Contents

The Bachelors and Widows Christmas Party

You might say Corrale was a typical village along the lonely stretch of highway east of Edmonton. A curling rink at one end and an agriplex at the other. A two-storey stucco hotel on the corner of main street that had seen better days, historic churches converted to housing or hardware stores, a postage-stamp-sized post office, and an Elk's Hall that doubled as a senior's drop-in during the week. A third of the roofs in town were in need of shingling, half the lawns full of kitsch (some of it more entertaining than others), with a slew of white pickups and the obligatory ram horns on their grills parked out front. Not much had changed in twenty, thirty, or even fifty years. Perhaps that's why residents looked forward to the few social (read: newsworthy) events of the year—the men to the annual Lazy Daze Rodeo and the women to the Bachelors and Widows Christmas Party.

It had been an annual tradition in Corrale since 1917, when Mel McConaghy and Adelaide Klapstein met, were smitten, engaged and married six months later, to have the seed of at least one union planted at the Bachelors and Widows Christmas Party. In fact, in those early years, there had been a dozen trysts a year, as reliable as a bouquet of daisies on Mother's Day. There had been so many settling in the country then, so many hopes. A farm on every quarter section, families of eight and ten. Childbirth, war, and gruelling work took their toll on people, not to mention the occasional epidemic. Hence there was always a plentiful supply of bereaved and unmarried men and women.

In recent years it had been harder and harder to even conjure one couple from the remnants of that past greatness. Most of the young people left Corrale at eighteen and never came back. The boys worked up in Fort McMurray or elsewhere in oil and gas. The girls went off to Edmonton or Calgary or Saskatoon to go to university or to work in an office tower.

Why, many young people never got married at all. They were so busy working, or forgot they were married and just drifted apart. But the chair of the organizing committee, Eva Waters had said to Bessie McCann that this year, 2017, the hundredth anniversary, was a do or die situation on all fronts—finances, attendance and matches—a crisis, and they had to do something.

In the past, the organizing committee had discussed ways of changing the name of the event to be more inclusive: one suggestion was to add *divorced and separated* to the moniker. A few years later a proposal was made to substitute Christmas with something less religious, such as *Holiday Match-Up*. Bessie said the first was too much of a mouthful, not to mention dour, and the second too crass. Even though most residents of Corrale didn't attend church or hold to religion of any kind anymore, Christmas was Christmas and always would be, forever, Amen. And, while no one would have said it out loud, deep down the Bachelors and Widows Christmas Party was regarded as a kind of omen for the year's proceedings, a modern-day rite if you will, for the prosperity of crops, of families, and the town. To some, *the party of all parties*. So, Eva suggested they do what all the banks did in the early 2000s and make the acronym, their brand. From then on the event was called: The B&W Xmas Party.

Early in the one hundredth year, Eva called a special meeting of the organizing committee. Even though they invited people from the four neighbouring communities, which they had since their seventy-fifth anniversary, this might be another year without an engagement, without a kindling of feeling of any kind. There was just nobody left. It might also be the year they lose their sponsorship from the Elks and the women's auxiliary, Order of the Royal Purple. They needed a new innovation, she said wringing her hands. Some kind of draw.

That is when Bessie hit upon the idea. "Maybe we've been focusing on the wrong group. Maybe the boomers are the gold mine. The ones on their retirement stoops."

"What do you mean?"

"Changing partners, living longer. Leverage all that."

"Okay." Eva was warming to the idea.

Bessie's eyes were shining. "What if we focus on people who went steady in high school but ended up marrying someone else? And then were divorced or widowed?"

Eva was nodding. "Like old friends who meet up after years and years and start right up again where they left off."

"A kick start to the romancing process!"

Eva sputtered, "But, but? What about the young people?"

"We make it a dual-purpose, hook-up and homecoming. Bring the family! Visit the old place. Stay a few days!"

Eva was sold.

That summer Bessie went through the local yearbooks and spent weeks on the internet with her granddaughter tracking down all the old names and flames, piecing together who went steady with whom, where they ended up and who might be newly eligible.

The out-of-towners in this category would get a special written invitation in their mailbox followed up by a phone call and the offer of a billet if needed. Local candidates would be approached over coffee by a friend, followed a week later by a phone call from the same friend reinforcing the message. Posters went up all over the county and neighbouring counties as in other years and even onto social media.

There were two potential couples that everyone's hopes were riding on.

Marshall Jackson had played junior hockey all through high school. Lena Williams worked two evenings a week at the local pharmacy. After they graduated from high school, Lena had wanted to study sciences at the university in Edmonton. It was not something a girl typically did in 1977. Marshall had wanted to play pro-hockey and that meant starting on farm teams, travelling and moving every year or two. Lena broke off the engagement.

Marshall never made it past the farm team. Instead, he ended up as a tool push not far from where he was born. From what Bessie could put together, Marshall had lived with a series of women, had children by one and grandchildren, but had never tied the knot. The rumour was that he had never really gotten over Lena. She had gone to university, met an ambitious medical student, got her degree, and married him. They had three children but Lena ended up widowed in her mid-thirties, her husband killed in a car crash. She had used the life insurance to train as a teacher and moved back home to be nearer her own family. When her children had grown, she had stepped into the principal role at the Corrale Elementary School and was still there.

There was hesitation, if not downright skepticism, about the second couple, Chester Malleck and Kate Orange, who in 1972, their final year, were top athlete and grad queen respectively and going steady. Their final evening together ended in a plate-throwing exercise for Kate because Chester had arrived an hour late and very drunk. Instead he had married an unremarkable self-effacing woman who had never raised her voice, made him supper every night without complaint, bore his children and passed in her sixties of breast cancer. He had often wondered out loud to friends if his life might have been more exciting if he had taken the other fork in the road, that is, the one leading to Kate. The word was they had been in touch on Facebook. His friends were honest: "You would have been dead in the ground like all her other husbands." The fact that she had outlived all four of her husbands, all of them dying from heart attacks, had occasioned the belief that Kate was a man killer.

But the B&W committee reasoned the two were a match in temperament and so, they were added to the special invitation list.

The festivities started on Friday, the second weekend of December. Things kicked off with the Mayor's breakfast and three tournaments designed to rekindle old links: pickle ball, shuffleboard and floor curling. Bessie offered to teach line dancing on the Friday night. It was an excuse for a little body contact and another reason for re-acquaintance before the big night to come. She started off with the *Hokey Pokey* (something easy).

"Shake that walker, now!

"Shake more bootie, all!"

"Come on, let's put your whole self in!"

Some grandchildren and great-grandchildren joined in, coaching their elders. Then Bessie moved on to *The Chicken Dance.*

"Ruffle those feathers! Let's have some woggle and a wiggle!"

She worked up the crowd to *Achy Breaky Heart* and a whole host of other country songs, ending the evening with *Fishing in the Dark.*

"Clap those hands, Pete! Jumping jacks! Heel and toe. That's right. Let's go, five, six, seven, eight!"

Bessie had everybody up and dancing even if their lines didn't always hold.

Mini-golf and floor curling filled the next day. Eva thought the turnout for the banquet Saturday night was stupendous. And though the moniker B&W Xmas Party had completely different origins, attendees, as they had in other years, dressed in black and white, with a splash of red thrown in for the season: a strand of garnets, a scarf, a pair of patent leather shoes, a pocket square, a tie or cuff links. The sea of suits and gowns made the evening positively glitter.

All the arriving ladies received a rose that night courtesy of AJ Auctioneers. Bessie and Eva did the honours, table to table, one carrying the box of corsages, the other, the pins. Graham Neary tried to fasten one on a slim, muscular woman's dress. Someone who looked vaguely familiar but almost no one recognized, and who sat unaccompanied at his table. She demurred to his thick paws.

"Why, that is so gentlemanly."

"What's your name?"

"Rhonda," she said. "Rhonda Lovett."

"Oh, I think I knew your brother, Ron. Some years behind me in school."

"Could be," she said. "No longer on the face of this earth. Moved on. Quite a few years back."

"Oh, I'm sorry. You must have been close in age." Graham's face had a punched in looked as if he were trying to work something out.

"Very close."

"Well, good to meet you." And he let his hand linger.

Eva poked Bessie. "Could this be?"

"Love at first sight?"

After the corsage-pinning ceremony, Rhonda had stretched out her long slim hand to each of her table mates in turn, making a grand show of the introductions. That's when the murmurs started.

"Ron Lovett had no sister," whispered Bessie. "We were in the same grade. There were no girls in that family."

"Look at that manicure. Her nails are perfect. And her body, her clothes—definitely a woman. Even her chin. No Adam's apple." Eva thought for a moment. "Do you suppose?"

Bessie's eyes lit up. "*Trans*—formed?"

"The full transition, I bet!" Eva clapped her hands together.

"I know those green eyes anywhere." Bessie winked.

The evening opened as it always did with a welcome from the Elks Exalted Ruler for the district, followed by an opening prayer from a man or woman of the cloth, this year the Lutherans. The hall was packed and the first course showcased devilled eggs. And these devils were serious: stuffed with sharp mustard and sprinkled with a generous dash of hot Hungarian paprika.

The organizers had taken something from each menu of the first five major anniversaries: ten years, twenty-five years, fifty years, sixty years, and seventy-five. The hors d'oeuvres were followed by French onion soup, the onions from Bailey's market garden caramelized to perfection, beef broth reduced from the bones of local herds, and croutons baked with gruyère from a local dairy. Onion soup was a stock course since the early days when it was hard to come by salad greens past the summer season and root vegetables kept well into February. Salad was the jellied tomato variety, perfected circa 1957 with just enough pickling spice to be considered exotic.

Main course was roast beef, gravy, potatoes with roasted Brussels sprouts, Yorkshire pudding and horseradish on the side for those who liked it. Although it was turkey season, the ladies auxiliary had taken to serving beef every year since the BSE crisis in 2003 as a sign of solidarity with the local cattle producers. Dessert was banana cream pie, one of the tropical fruits that made it to small towns a hundred years ago, mixed with eggs and farm fresh cream.

There were speeches over dessert, percolated coffee served, and squares and tarts, all designed to make people linger. The raffle for the trip for two to Hawaii would come at midnight with a hundred or so consolation prizes thrown in: a cast iron pot and pan set, top-of-the-line power tools, a leather golf cart, flashlights, work gloves, umbrellas, and quarts of motor oil. A spa day package, gift certificate from a local restaurant, and another from a greenhouse. Even a few miniature tea sets and Lego and train sets that might be re-gifted to the grandchildren.

For Chester, the menu was the first mistake. True to B&W tradition, no one had bothered to check for dietary restrictions or preferences. Chester didn't like onions. He left his bowl aside and wouldn't even sip on the broth. It reminded Kate why she had dumped him in the first place. Not only did she not want to live a life without onions (the closest thing to a spice in these parts), but she did not want to live with someone who was picky about what he ate. Because if he was picky about that, he was likely picky about the neighbourhood they might live in, the house they might buy—and about her too. Which was the real reason, she'd realized now, she had thrown plates at him all those decades ago.

From that point on in the evening, Kate ignored him, except to ask if she could eat his soup, which he wasn't touching and which he handed to her with a curt Hmmp! She pointedly amused herself with her old high school friend, Thelma McConaghy, talking quilts and documentaries.

16

At the other table, disaster had also struck. Marshall, who wasn't much used to suits and ties, and whose hands were numb from arthritis after years of working in the oil patch, had managed to splash onion broth on his pressed white shirt. He had tried to angle his tie over the place, but still it showed. Lena reacted quickly, asking the waiter for a couple of extra cloth napkins and a glass of cold water. Between him unbuttoning his shirt, stuffing a dry napkin behind, and her daubing the stain with a wet napkin, Marshall remembered the thrill he used to have seeing her on a date.

Eva noticed that Marshall turned positively chatty. He asked after Lena's family and pastimes. He ate with perfect grace for the rest of the evening and even spoke of his ex-loves with a certain fondness and his two daughters with a tear in his eye. They had all made good matches and the grandchildren were teenagers already, some of them. Once and a while now that he was retired he spent a few days with them, cooking breakfast, playing street hockey, and even gotten hooked on reading *Twilight*, which started a fit of giggles in Lena that she could not stop. Marshall was grinning from ear to ear. "You haven't changed, Lena. You always took care of yourself."

"Do you still play the game?" Lena asked.

"Oh sure, some old-timers leagues. Full gear, helmets and no checking."

Marshall ventured a few queries about her grandchildren and about retirement.

Wasn't she thinking of hanging up the spurs?

"Maybe next year," she responded. "I think I'm still a good teacher and even a better principal."

He liked her spunk and his face showed it.

What did he do in his spare time?

"Cooking," Marshall said. He even baked his own bread. He had never cooked for himself before. On the road for work all the time. Camp jobs. He'd never really learned how, but now he liked it. And he liked to have company, he added.

A small twinkle entered Lena's eye. "I would never have seen you as house husband material." He almost lost his pie laughing.

"Actually I have to credit my daughters. They were the ones who said to me when I got the diabetes diagnosis, 'Dad you've got to learn how to take care of yourself.' And the doctor who told me I had to cut out the fast food if I wanted to live long enough to see my grandchildren. So I did. Took up the gym, too, a few times a week. And walking. Now I'm retired, I walk everywhere. Got my blood sugar count down to normal without medication."

"That's quite a change for you. All those model cars you used to mail order when we were going out. Not to mention the actual wrecks. What was the one you were rebuilding in your dad's garage when we were in Grade 12?"

Lena closed her eyes trying to recollect.

"The '64 Chevy Malibu convertible."

"That's right."

"Sold that a few years back. Became a liability with all this divorcing and moving around."

Lena was smiling, her hand under her chin. A sure sign to everyone who was watching that she was seriously sizing him up as mate material. As the folklore goes, while man may be the hunter, woman makes the final choice.

Across the room the top athlete and the grad queen were doing less well. After Kate's friend wandered off to the ladies room, Chester had seized the opportunity to talk and talk about his grandchildren, none of whom were present. How one was articling in a very old law firm in the city, another was competing in provincial figure skating trials and another big in the IT world. They'd all, at least by his reckoning, ended up prospering in some fashion.

"But what do you do in your spare time now, Chester?"

"Watch golf. On television. Live. Hours and hours a week. Can't get enough of it."

He laughed easily.

The years had filled Chester out so much that Kate could no longer see the track and field champ in his ill-fitting suit. A frown passed over her face.

Chester pressed on undaunted. "The knees are brand spanking new. I had surgery last year, but now I need an operation on this hip to get back on the course," he said, pointing to the offending bone. "I'm lucky I can walk at all these days. Hasn't stopped me from getting around though. I've rigged up a recumbent bicycle and some days in summer I ride everywhere with that. Downtown Lacombe, around the lakes, all around the course. I even run the dogs on it. Makes me feel like a kid again."

Kate imagined herself riding along beside him and her frown deepened.

He didn't dance anymore either. Too hard on the hip. Even the slow ones. He smiled. But he liked to watch. Kate did not smile back at him.

Eva had her eye on Graham and Rhonda. "Our love-at-first-sight-couple is getting along like a house on fire!"

"Or is it second-sight?" Bessie whispered and they both giggled.

Graham Neary was one of the original bachelors. A confirmed bachelor everyone said, but Rhonda had him laughing and smiling and talking all about himself.

When Bessie edged closer to their table to take their dinner plates, she heard them discussing how to put a snowmobile engine together.

Rhonda managed a fashion boutique about halfway between the two most expensive clothing stores in downtown Calgary. "My prices are about half. I get women coming out of both who don't want to pay six hundred dollars for a bit of skirt that fits them badly. I take them in, work with them, focus on their self-esteem. One dressing room. Stock covering every square inch of the store. Good quality middle-American brands. That's all they need. A little attention."

Graham Neary was listening with admiration. He fancied himself a shrewd business man. "I used to run the farm supply in town. Cut back last year though. Semi-retired. Help out when I can, but I still have way too much time on my hands."

At the first dance Marshall didn't hesitate to ask Lena. He noticed how they could still dance in sync. It was like they had never stopped. Her weight, her leaning into him like that. His arm firm, step sure.

By the witching hour, what they call midnight in Corrale, the athlete and the queen had left and gone their separate ways. Across the room, Marshall and Lena sat beside each other with his shoulder lightly pressed against hers, their heads leaning into each other, joking about the haul of raffle prizes on the stage and for the next hour listening to the caller, a middle-aged woman with a good singing voice, make running commentary on the prizes and how the recipient might enjoy them: *Hal, you could use this bubble bath, soften your skin, make you smell real pretty. Jim, you could use a manicure—this will come in handy!* And so on. This went on till the Grand Prize Draw was announced. The trip for two to Hawaii went to one of the bachelors in the room who came, as most did every year, for the food and the entertainment, no hopes of a match with anyone.

Through all the dancing and the raffle calling, Rhonda and Graham kept talking. Rhonda had her pilot's license. So did Graham. They were swapping airplane stories. One seater versus two seater. Wheels versus float planes.

Bessie had to move on to the next table but she kept her good ear cocked.

Rhonda said she just went up for fun, how it made her feel good to look down on everything, the world spread out, so much still wild. "All that prairie. Rivers and mountain lakes. Like at the beginning of time."

"Well, you must come up with me some time. Be my co-pilot." Bessie saw him slip her his card.

Eva was gobsmacked. "Well I'll be."

"The dark horse in the race," Bessie agreed, and the marker of yet another successful year of the B&W Xmas Party. So when word got back to the organizing committee that Marshall and Lena had booked their own trip to Hawaii, Eva and Bessie congratulated themselves on making at least two new matches that year. For a trip weighed about the same these days as a wedding ceremony as a sign of commitment. Yet those weren't the only signs. Some of the young people newly met were seen exchanging phone numbers and sparky looks in the parking lot at the end of the weekend. "A good omen for next year," said Bessie.

At the end of it all, Eva reckoned the committee had truly come into the twenty-first century and the B&W Xmas Party survived to live another year. Now, every year, they put a big note at the bottom of their posters:

EVERYONE WELCOME

And according to Bessie and Eva, it worked every time.

ACKNOWLEDGEMENTS

Thanks to my friend Susan Beach who alerted me to the quaint and endearing tradition of the bachelor and widows Christmas party. Everything else I made up! Several people read first drafts of this story: Barbara Geiger, Darrin Hagen, Betty Jane Hegerat, and Elisabeth Hegerat. Finally, thanks to Lexie Angelo for her close read and fine editing of the story.

ABOUT THE AUTHOR

Audrey J. Whitson was the 30th Writer in Residence at MacEwan University in 2023. Her novel, *The Death of Annie the Water Witcher by Lightning*, was a finalist for the Robert Kroetsch City of Edmonton Book Prize in 2020. Audrey's collection of coming-of-age stories, *The Glorious Mysteries*, was longlisted for the 2014 Frank O'Connor International Short Story Award. Her memoir, *Teaching Places*, was shortlisted for three awards in 2004, including the Grant MacEwan Authors Award. Audrey lives in amiskwacîwâskahikan (also known as Edmonton), in Treaty 6 territory. To learn more about her blog and her books, visit www.audreywhitson.com

SPECIAL THANKS

Calgary Arts Development

Calgary Public Library

IngramSpark